GUNNE

Story of a Bombing R

Dee Phillips

D1427923

READZONE

First published in this edition 2013

ReadZone Books Limited
50 Godfrey Avenue
Twickenham
TW2 7PF
UK

All rights reserved. No part of this publication may be reproduced, stored in a retrieval system, or transmitted, in any form, or by any means, electronic, mechanical, photocopying, or otherwise, without the prior permission of ReadZone Books Limited

© **Copyright Ruby Tuesday Books Limited 2013**
© **Copyright in this edition ReadZone Books 2013**

The right of the Author to be identified as the Author of this work has been asserted by the Author in accordance with the Copyright, Designs and Patents Act 1988

Every attempt has been made by the Publisher to secure appropriate permissions for material reproduced in this book. If there has been any oversight we will be happy to rectify the situation in future editions or reprints. Written submissions should be made to the Publishers.

British Library Cataloguing in Publication Data (CIP) is available for this title.

ISBN 978-1-78322-011-3

Printed in China

Developed and Created by Ruby Tuesday Books Ltd
Project Director – Ruth Owen
Designer – Elaine Wilkinson

Images courtesy of public domain, Shutterstock and Superstock (pages 24–25, 32–33).

Acknowledgements
With thanks to Lorraine Petersen, Chief Executive of NASEN, for her help in the development and creation of these books

Visit our website: www.readzonebooks.com

The drone of the engines fills my ears.
The same thought goes around
and around in my head.

Will I die tonight?

TAIL GUNNER
The Story of a Bombing Raid

During World War II, Britain's Bomber Command Force flew bombing raids over Germany.

Night after night, they bombed German factories where weapons and aircraft were being made.

German anti-aircraft guns on the ground shot at the bombers.

Enemy fighter planes, known as night fighters, tried to blow them out of the skies.

About 125,000 men joined Bomber Command.

More than **55,000** lost their **lives.**

The drone of the engines
fills my ears.
We fly on through the dark night.

Please, God.
Let us make it back.

Please don't let it be us tonight.

The drone of the engines fills my ears.
I peer out into the darkness.
I watch for night fighters.
I have to keep us safe.
Jim, Archie, Will, Gibby, Frankie, CJ and me.

Please, God.
Don't let it be us tonight.

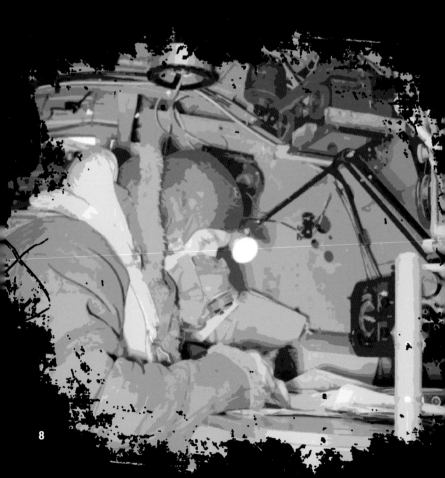

I was 18 when I joined up.
I wanted to be on a bomber crew.
Taking the fight to the Germans.

I wanted to be a tail gunner.
Keeping the plane safe.
Keeping my mates safe.

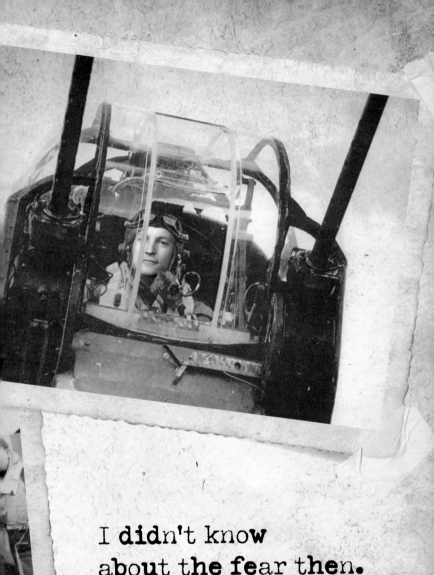

I didn't know
about the fear then.

There are no words for the fear.
So you keep it deep inside you.

Will I die tonight?
That's the fear.

The drone of the engines fills my ears.
It's so very cold up here.
Here in the tail gunner's turret.
I'm crushed into this tiny space.
I can't move my legs.
My breath freezes into an icicle.

The same thought goes around and around in my head.
Will I die tonight?

We fly on through the dark night.
Heading for Germany.
Archie and I watch for night fighters.
A small flash of light.
A dark shape.
An enemy fighter plane that will
blow us out of the sky.

Hour after cold hour passes.
Suddenly,

BANG!
BANG! BANG!

German guns on the ground.
We're taking flak.

Red and orange flashes all around us.

I hear Frankie from the cockpit.
He's the flight engineer.
His voice comes through
my headphones.
"We're hit, but we're ok."

Sweat pours from my face.
My stomach churns.

There are no words for the fear.
But we cannot turn back.

Now I feel the plane slowing.
We're over our target.

I hear Gibby through my headphones.
He's the bomb aimer.
He's in the plane's nose.

Gibby says to Jim the pilot,
"Hold her steady."
"Steady. Steady. Straight."
Then finally, "Bombs away!"

Below us our bombs become a sea of fire.
I try not to think of the people below.
Men. Women. Children. Babies.

I wanted to take the fight to the Germans.

But I don't know any more.

We fly on through the dark night.
Heading for home.
Then suddenly, I see it.
Off to our left.
A night fighter.

My fingers get ready on the triggers.
Has he seen us? Should I fire?

I shout, "Corkscrew! Corkscrew!"

Jim takes the plane down,
down in a steep dive.
Then up and up.

Sweat pours from my face.
My stomach churns.

Did he see us?
Did we get out of view in time?

I peer out into the darkness.
But nothing.
Tonight will not be our night to die.

But I've seen it, you see.

I've seen how it goes for the lads
who don't make it back.

There were dozens of us bombers
on that summer evening.
All heading for Germany.
Then I saw the night fighter.

He was under their plane.
I saw the flashes of his guns.
Then the huge ball of fire.

FALLING!

FALLING!

FALLING!

Lads like us.
Lads like me.
Falling to earth in a ball of fire.

I knew those lads.
They shared our hut.
Seven empty bunks.
A half-written letter to
a sweetheart.
A game of chess never finished.

Lads like me that didn't
make it back.

My Darling Peggy,

How are you

The sun is coming up as we climb from our plane.

There are no words for the fear.
So we say nothing.
We light cigarettes.
We look at the holes in our plane.

We walk slowly back to our hut.
Jim, Archie, Will, Gibby, Frankie, CJ and me.

Tonight was not our night to die.
This time we made it back.

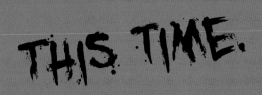

THIS TIME.

Tail Gunner:

Behind the Story

During World War II, Britain launched a massive bombing campaign to destroy Germany's ability to make weapons and build aircraft. Bomber Command Force was set up to drop bombs on targets in Germany and countries where Germany was in control.

Many of the bomber crews flew Lancaster bombers. A seven-man crew was made up of a pilot, a flight engineer, a bomb aimer, a radio operator, two gunners and a navigator who used maps and a compass to find the crew's targets. A bombing mission might last for 10 hours. The planes flew in total darkness, while the gunners kept watch for enemy fighter planes.

A Bomber Command crew would fly up to 40 missions before they were released from their duties. Many crews were killed on their

A Lancaster bomber

first mission. Others were shot down after 10 or 20 missions. The terrifying fact was that, on any given night, it was simply a matter of luck as to whether or not you made it back.

The aim of Bomber Command's campaign was to destroy Germany's industry. Thousands of civilians living in the areas close to the factories were killed, however. During the war and in the years since, many people have questioned if the bombing was right. Others argue that without Bomber Command, Germany would not have been defeated.

Whatever your feelings, the bravery shown by the thousands of young men who did their duty is truly astounding.

Tail Gunner – *What's next?*

GOOD LUCK CHARM
ON YOUR OWN / IN A GROUP

Most of the men of Bomber Command carried something with them for luck. It might have been a letter from home, a silk stocking from a sweetheart or even an enemy bullet that had once missed them on an earlier bombing raid!

- If you had to choose one precious or lucky item to carry with you into a dangerous situation what would it be?

THAT'S THE FEAR
ON YOUR OWN / WITH A PARTNER / IN A GROUP

The tail gunner's fear is, "Will I die tonight?"

Think of a time when you were afraid. Try to remember how your fear felt. Write down words or phrases that describe your feelings at that time. Then try organising them into a short poem.

Mum's operation
Sick feeling
Will Mum die?
Cold waiting room
It's not fair
Hate the hospital

BOMBS AWAY
WITH A PARTNER

The bomb aimer had to guide the pilot over the plane's target by speaking directions. Play this game to see if you can guide a partner using just your voice.

- Ask your partner to put on a blindfold.

- Place a plastic bowl on the ground away from your partner. Hand your partner a ball.

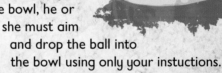

- Now direct your partner to the bowl using only your voice. When your partner reaches the bowl, he or she must aim and drop the ball into the bowl using only your instuctions.

BOOK TALK
IN A GROUP

The tail gunner and his crew are characters in a story. Their story, however, is based on what happened to thousands of men who flew with Bomber Command Force. Discuss with your group how the story and the facts you've learned make you feel. Think about:

- How did the men cope with their fear of being killed? And the loss of friends who lived alongside them?

- Try to imagine how it felt to carry out a mission knowing your bombs would kill people on the ground.

Titles in the
Yesterday's Voices
series

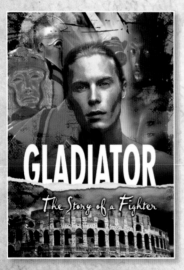

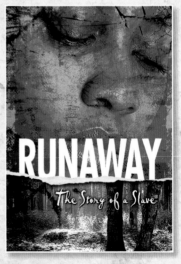

I waited deep below the arena.
Then it was my turn to fight.
Kill or be killed!

I cannot live as a slave
any longer. Tonight, I will
escape and never go back.

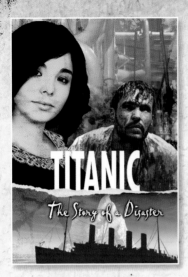

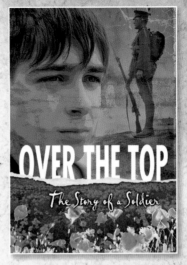

TITANIC
The Story of a Disaster

OVER THE TOP
The Story of a Soldier

The ship is sinking into the icy sea. I don't want to die. Someone help us!

I'm waiting in the trench. I am so afraid. Tomorrow, we go over the top.

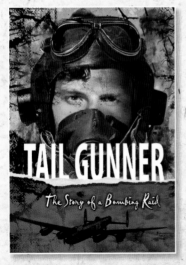

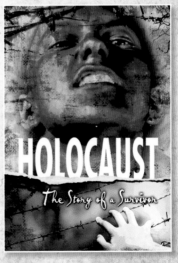

TAIL GUNNER
The Story of a Bombing Raid

HOLOCAUST
The Story of a Survivor

Another night. Another bombing raid. Will this night be the one when we don't make it back?

They took my clothes and shaved my head. I was no longer a human.